ELePhant
White

garden Shed

Lucy finds
Elephant

living room

dining roo

kitchen

The bird bath

Elephant White
leaves home

The Pagoda

garden bench

TV room

bathroom

Lucy's
bedroom

hall

utility room

entrance

Lucy's
parents'
bedroom

The Pond

Written by
Will Brenton

Illustrated by
Holly Clifton-Brown

ELePhant
White

templar publishing
www.templarco.co.uk

LUCY and ELEPHANT WHITE loved playing their own special games, ringing bluebells, catching splashes and playing 'Hide and Hide' (so nobody ever found them).

"Oh, Elephant White!" cried Lucy. "You're so patchy-white and wonderful. I love you! You are my best friend in the whole wide world." And she gave him her very cosiest cuddle.

Then the doorbell rang.

"It's Aunt Lizzie," called Mum.
"She's brought you a present."
Lucy tore the paper away.
"A Crystal Fairy!" she cried. "She's beautiful."

Mum smiled. "Treat her carefully — she's very precious!"
Lucy played with Crystal Fairy all day long.
Sitting alone in a corner, Elephant White watched the
galaxy of sparkles she brought to Lucy's wide eyes.
"I'm not very precious," he thought.

That night, beneath the silver Spring moon, as the stars
cheekily twinkled and Lucy lay dreaming of candyfloss dragons,
Elephant White climbed out of the window.
He jumped onto a nearby branch, tip-toed down through
the apple blossom and then turned to look back at the house.
"I need to find a place I might fit just right,"
sighed Elephant White, and sadly walked away.

After quite some time, Elephant White
came across a huge red and white tent —
the Big Top, home to the famous Mouse Circus!
"I can use an Elephant like you,"
said the Ringmaster as soon as he saw him.
"I'll make you the star of our show!"

So Elephant White pulled on a pair of baggy
trousers, painted his trunk red and
rolled it up into a big round nose...

At the grand finale
the band played a long drum roll
and the crowd held their breath...

Elephant White climbed to the top of
the mouse pyramid and stood on one leg!
"Bravo!" the crowd called. "Encore! Encore!"
Elephant White puffed up with pride and decided to wave.

Disaster!

The mice
wavered and wobbled, swayed and swaggered...
and they all came tumbling down!
"That elephant is too big for the Big Top!"
cried the Ringmaster.

Later, beneath a golden summer moon,
as the Mouse Clowns rehearsed their Shakespeare
and the Trapeze Mice dreamed of flying with real wings,
Elephant White looked back at the Big Top.

"I need to find a place I might fit just right,"
sighed Elephant White, and sadly walked away.

After quite some time, Elephant White
came to the shores of a great greeny-blue sea.
There he spied a black and white galleon —
the ship of the Badger Pirates!

"I can use a fellow like ye!" bellowed Captain Beardy.
"Step aboard and join my crew!"

The Jolly Badger

But, as Elephant White carefully walked up the gang plank...

disaster!

The ship shuddered and shook...
creaked and cracked, pitched and plunged, and began to sink!

"That elephant is too vast for this vessel!"
blustered the Captain, as they all started bailing out the water.

Later, beneath the tumbling Autumn leaves,
as the Captain and his pirates practised
their ballroom dancing, Elephant White
crept away from the shore.

"I need to find a place I might fit just right," sighed Elephant White, and sadly walked away.

After quite some time, he came to a roaring waterfall, where brave bright red pilots flew through sheets of water.

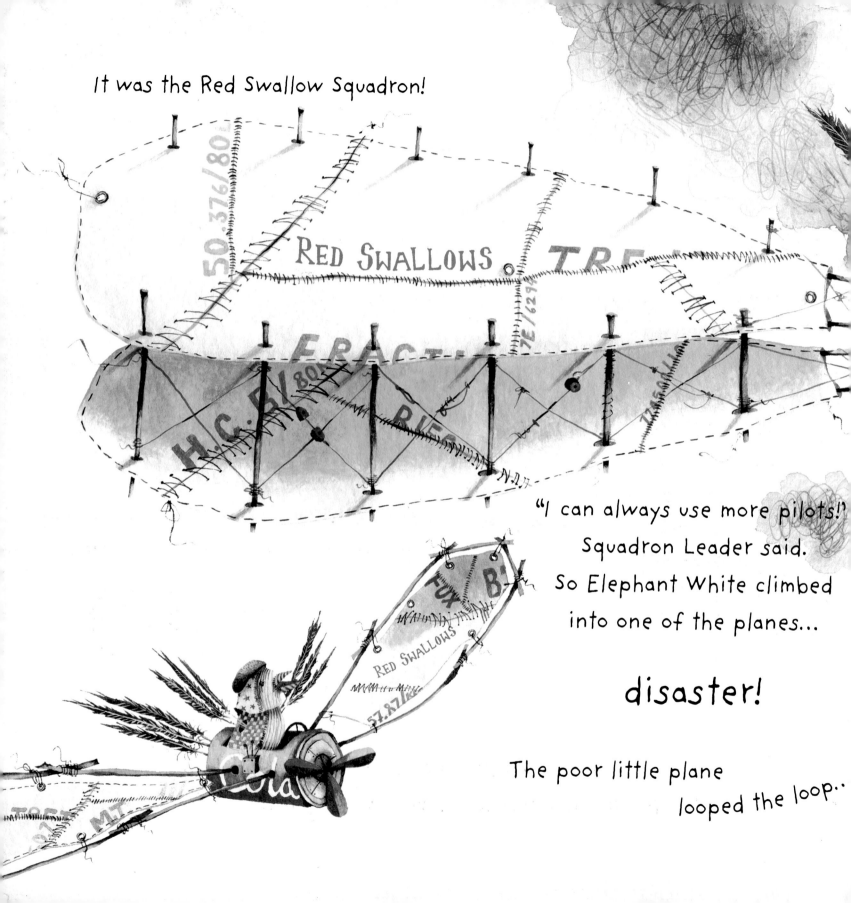

It was the Red Swallow Squadron!

"I can always use more pilots!"
Squadron Leader said.
So Elephant White climbed
into one of the planes...

disaster!

The poor little plane
looped the loop...

then rolled and flopped...

and coughed and dropped!

Elephant White leaped out
and floated in his parachute towards the ground.

Later, beneath a pale
Winter moon, as the swallows
played statues and imagined a life
that didn't pass by in a fluttering flash,
Elephant White stared back up
into the skies, feeling lost
and alone.

"It seems there's nowhere that I might fit just right," sighed Elephant White. He curled his trunk around his cold toes and sank into the snow.

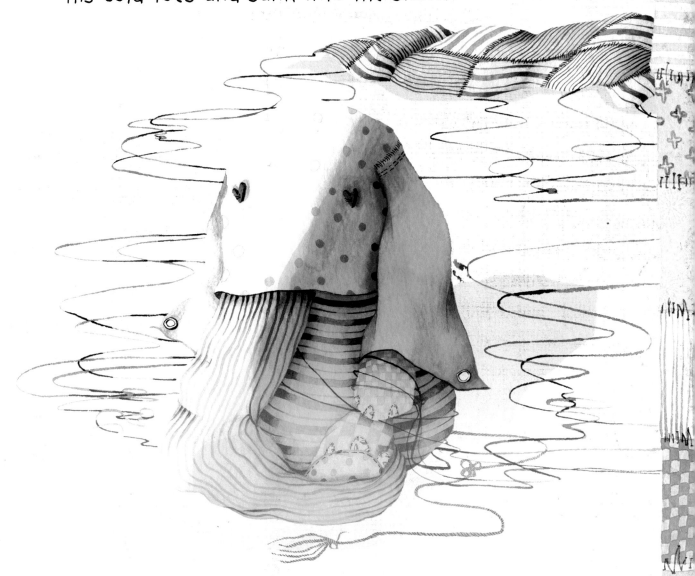

But then he heard a familiar voice...

"Elephant White — you've come home!"
And there was Lucy, her face full of smiles.

Lucy picked up Elephant White and held him very, very tight.
"Oh, Elephant White! Where did you go?"
Elephant White whispered tales of trapeze mice,
dancing pirates and swooping swallows.

Lucy laughed. "Elephant White, you are the most precious thing
in the world! How I've missed your stories!"

"More precious than Crystal Fairy?" asked Elephant White.
"Much more precious than all the crystal fairies in the world,"
said Lucy, and she gave him her very cosiest cuddle.

For Ella and Boo ~ Will
For Ellie & Molly Moo ~ Holly

A TEMPLAR BOOK

First published in the UK in 2012 by Templar Publishing,
an imprint of The Templar Company Limited,
The Granary, North Street, Dorking, Surrey, RH4 1DN, UK
www.templarco.co.uk

First edition

ISBN 978-1-84877-590-9

Printed in China